A Crazy Case of
ROBOTS

Other books by Kenneth Oppel

Barnes and the Brains Series:
A Bad Case of Ghosts
A Strange Case of Magic
A Crazy Case of Robots
*An Incredible Case of Dinosaurs**
*A Weird Case of Super-Goo**
Emma's Emu
Silverwing
Sunwing
The Live-Forever Machine
Dead Water Zone
Peg and the Whale
Follow that Star

* forthcoming

A Crazy Case of

ROBOTS

KENNETH OPPEL

Illustrated by
Sam Sisco

Scholastic Canada Ltd.

Scholastic Canada Ltd.
175 Hillmount Rd., Markham, Ontario, Canada L6C 1Z7

Scholastic Inc.
555 Broadway, New York, NY 10012, USA

Scholastic Australia Pty Limited
PO Box 579, Gosford, NSW 2250, Australia

Scholastic New Zealand Ltd.
Private Bag 94407, Greenmount, Auckland,
New Zealand

Scholastic Publications Ltd.
Villiers House, Clarendon Avenue, Leamington Spa,
Warwickshire CV32 5PR, UK

Canadian Cataloguing in Publication Data

Oppel, Kenneth
  A crazy case of robots

(Barnes and the brains)
ISBN 0-439-98824-1

I. Sisco, Sam. II. Title. III. Series: Oppel, Kenneth. Barnes and the brains.

PS8579.P64C72 2001   jC813'.54   C00-932491-7
PZ7.O66Cr 2001

6 5 4 3 2 1   Printed in Canada   1 2 3 4 5/0

For Graham Mills.

Contents

Chapter 1

Danger! High Voltage!

"KEVIN AND TINA QUARK! Local geniuses!"

Giles Barnes smiled to himself as he weaved through the crowds at the school science fair. He recognized Kevin's voice instantly, even though he couldn't see him yet.

The gymnasium was packed. It was difficult for Giles to even get close to some of the displays. So far he'd seen five entries on dinosaurs, three on volcanoes, one on optical illusions, and another on venus flytraps. He'd also seen an enterprising girl dressed up as an electron, whirling around the gymnasium and crashing into people. It was causing quite a stir.

"Local geniuses!" came Kevin's voice again, rising

above the general din. "Capable of just about anything! Reasonable rates!"

Giles steered around a knot of people and finally caught a glimpse of a boy with curly red hair and a face splotched with freckles. He was standing in the middle of the aisle, trying to hand out business cards to passersby.

"Hi, Kevin!" Giles called out, drawing closer. "Drumming up some customers?"

"Public relations," said Kevin wisely. "That's the key, Barnes. Good public relations. And this is the perfect place for it. Look at all these people! Oh, hang on a second!"

Kevin swivelled around to face an elderly man sidling past. "Excuse me, sir," he said, offering him one of the business cards. "My name's Kevin Quark and I'm a local genius and — "

The man hurried by without taking a card.

"His loss," said Kevin with a shrug. "Let me tell you, Barnes, it's not easy being a genius."

Giles nodded, hoping he looked sympathetic. He'd never forget the first time he met Tina and Kevin Quark. They'd appeared on his doorstep, introduced themselves as geniuses, and told him there was a good chance his house was haunted.

Since then his life simply hadn't been the same.

It might be difficult being a genius, Giles thought. But what about being the *friend* of geniuses? He couldn't remember the last time Tina had made a mistake in class. She could memorize whole pages from the encyclopedia. She could divide huge numbers faster than a pocket calculator. She even knew how to program her parents' video machine! And Tina and Kevin always seemed to be cooking up some new invention for their genius business — fantastic contraptions that shot out sparks and steam and made shrill beeping noises.

"Wait until you see our science fair entry," Kevin told Giles proudly.

"Where is it?"

"Well, the thing is," said Kevin, lowering his voice, "it's not quite ready yet. Tina's still working on it. Some last minute touches. I'm a little worried it won't be finished in time. But come on, I'll show you."

Kevin led the way through the throng to Tina's booth.

Giles frowned.

"What's going on?" he said in bewilderment.

The booth was completely barricaded with large

sheets of cardboard. Written across the outside in fierce black letters was DO NOT DISTURB, and TRESPASSERS WILL BE PROSECUTED, as well as DANGER! HIGH VOLTAGE!

"Tina's taking this awfully seriously, isn't she?" Giles asked.

Orange light flashed through the gaps in the cardboard, accompanied by sharp crackling noises. Then came a high-pitched drilling sound.

"It seems she has some fairly big equipment in there," said Giles.

Kevin nodded in admiration.

"So, what is it?" Giles asked.

"Well I, um, don't know, to tell you the truth," Kevin replied, his face colouring. "She wouldn't even let me help out on this one. I've been banned from the workshop altogether for the last two weeks!"

"It must be something pretty special," said Giles.

"It makes sense, I suppose," said Kevin matter-of-factly. "After all, I'm only a little bit of a genius, so I can't expect her to let me in on all the inventions."

But Giles couldn't help noticing that Kevin looked a little hurt.

Quite a crowd had gathered around by this time, and whenever a puff of smoke drifted up into the air, or an electric snap sounded, there were *oohs* and *ahhhs* from the audience, as if it were all some marvellous fireworks show.

Kevin tapped respectfully on the cardboard.

"Tina?" he said.

"Who's there?" came a muffled voice.

"It's Kevin."

"Kevin who?"

"Kevin Quark, your brother!"

After a moment, Tina squeezed out between two panels of cardboard. She was very tiny, with precise blond braids hanging on either side of her head. There was a smudge of grease across her cheek.

"Good day, Barnes," she said with a perfunctory nod.

"Hello, O Great One," said Giles with a grin.

"How's it going in there?" Kevin asked.

"I'm finished," Tina replied. A small smile shifted across her lips as she looked around. "I see we have quite an audience. Well, I hardly think anyone will be disappointed."

People were jockeying for position around the booth, standing on tiptoe, rocking their heads from side to side, hoping for a good glimpse of what was behind the barricade.

"What's going on in there?" someone asked.

"Is it alive?" another wanted to know.

"Is it dangerous?"

"Is it fit for children to see?"

"Stand back everyone, please!" said Tina.

With a flourish, she pulled a long piece of twine, and with an airy sigh, the walls of the cardboard barricade fell gracefully outwards to the floor.

Everyone gasped.

A robot.

Chapter 2

Tinatron

"LADIES AND GENTLEMEN," Tina proclaimed, "this is the Tinatron 1000!"

Giles took a few steps closer for a better look.

The robot was roughly the same size as Tina. Gauges and switches covered its boxy metal chest. Two spindly metal arms jutted from its sides, each with a rubber-glove hand at the end. Tinatron's head was long and rectangular, with what looked like a flashlight and a camera lens for eyes, and for a mouth, the speaker of a portable CD player.

Two thick silver cables connected the robot's head to the top of its chest. Giles didn't know what its legs looked like, because they were hidden beneath a kind of metal skirt that extended almost to the floor. Poking out from the bottom was a pair of mismatched running shoes.

"Hey!" said Kevin, pointing at the robot's head. "That's my camera!"

"As a matter of fact, it is," said Tina. "It was perfect for my purposes."

"And that's my CD player, too!" Kevin exclaimed.

"Kevin, please," said Tina. "You're making a scene."

"You could have asked! I've been looking for that stuff!"

"You should be delighted that I've been able to make use of it in such a remarkable invention."

"But why does it always have to be *my* stuff?" Kevin wanted to know.

Tina pretended not to hear.

"Where did you get all the other parts?" asked Giles.

"The metal salvage yard down by the river. There's a wealth of raw material there."

Giles imagined Tina, skulking around with a flashlight at night like a grave robber, pocketing automobile parts and bits of gutted TVs.

"Does it talk?" someone in the audience wanted to know.

8

Tina smiled indulgently and turned to the robot.

"Introduce yourself," Tina said to it.

"Good morning," said the robot in a strange, metallic voice. "I am Tinatron 1000, created by Tina Quark. I am a high-performance, low-maintenance, super-efficient, multi-purpose, hyper-intelligent robot. I am programmed to perform any task without error."

The audience hummed in amazement.

"Its voice!" Kevin hissed to Giles. "It sounds — "

"I know," said Giles. "It sounds a little like Tina's."

"Spooky, isn't it?"

"Very."

Giles couldn't help thinking that the robot even *looked* a little bit like Tina. The two silver cables that dangled from its metal head weren't so unlike Tina's blond braids. And there was even something similar about the way the robot stood, very straight and serious, its hands folded calmly together in front.

"I will now give a demonstration of Tinatron 1000's abilities," announced Tina grandly.

She ordered the robot to balance on one of its metal legs, then to pick up eggs without breaking them. She asked the robot to multiply large numbers and write the answers in clear handwriting on a chalkboard. Then Tina invited the audience to ask Tinatron anything it wished. The robot answered questions on astrophysics, ancient history, and biochemistry. It did not make a single mistake.

"May I may have everyone's attention, please!"

Giles turned to look at the stage. Mr. Lunardi, the school science teacher, was speaking into a microphone.

"It is now time to announce this year's science fair winner. The judges and I have seen some very impressive entries today, but there is one entry which we feel surpasses all others. I would like to ask Tina Quark to come to the stage and accept first prize!"

"But what about me?" said Kevin. "I thought we were partners!"

But Tina was already marching up to the front, the robot keeping pace at her side. Mr. Lunardi looked a little taken aback as Tinatron expertly climbed the steps to the stage and extended its rubber-glove hand for the trophy. Mr. Lunardi hesitated for a moment, and then handed it over. As Tina stood by, smiling faintly, the robot gently pushed Mr. Lunardi away from the microphone.

"This is a great honour," said the robot. "Thank you very much indeed."

The gymnasium erupted into more applause. Cameras flashed.

"Sometimes it makes you want to gag, doesn't it?" said Kevin to Giles.

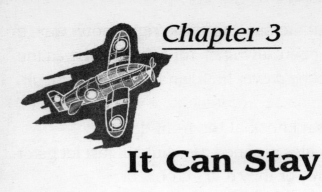

Chapter 3

It Can Stay

GILES DABBED SOME MODEL GLUE onto the edges of the two plastic pieces, and pressed them firmly together.

From the ceiling of his bedroom hung an assortment of model airplanes. There were modern jet fighters and old fashioned biplanes, huge 747s and angular spaceships. Giles took great pride in his collection. He wasn't one of those model builders who simply slapped them together, forcing parts, leaving globs of glue oozing between joints to harden. He took his time. He'd learned that patience was absolutely essential.

Tina and Kevin might be geniuses, but he was a master model builder.

Spread out across his desk right now was a bomber he'd been saving up for for ages. It was the biggest model he'd ever built, and the most difficult, too.

There was a knock at the front door.

"Typical," Giles groaned. He couldn't just let go of the pieces now, or they'd dry crooked.

Another knock.

His father, he knew, was out back in his workshop, going over the plans for home renovations. And his mother was in her study, with the door tightly shut, working on some huge math equation to torture her university students with.

He sighed. It would have to be him. He carefully put down the pieces and thumped downstairs.

It was Kevin and Tina, both looking rather awkward. Behind them stood the robot.

"I was in the middle of something," Giles said a little testily.

"Good afternoon, Barnes," said Tina. "We seem to have a bit of a problem."

"You do?"

Giles wondered what it could possibly be. Just this morning Tina had won first prize in the science fair, everyone had called her a genius, and her picture would undoubtedly be splashed all over the local newspapers tomorrow morning. She'd probably be invited to take part in the next space launch, and knighted by the Queen before the school year ended! What could the problem be?

"Mom won't have the robot in the house," Kevin explained simply.

"Why not?" Giles said.

"She thinks it's off-putting," said Tina, rolling her eyes.

"She thinks it's inhuman," said Kevin.

"She thinks it's unwholesome," said Tina.

"She thinks it's a lot of things," added Kevin in confidential tones, "but I won't repeat them here. They're kind of nasty."

"What we're wondering, Barnes," began Tina, avoiding his eyes, "is if you might possibly do us just a little bit of a favour — not much of a favour really, just a very small one." She paused to take a deep breath. "Could you let Tinatron stay here, while we give Mom a chance to calm down?"

Giles glanced at the robot, standing very still and serious behind the two Quarks.

"Well, I can ask," said Giles uncertainly. "But I don't think my parents are going to be too pleased.

You know how my mom is about your inventions, Tina — especially after that incident with the super carpet cleaner."

"Ah, yes," said Tina, pursing her lips and frowning as if it had all happened a very long time ago. "That was somewhat of a disappointment, wasn't it?"

"Our carpet used to be blue," said Giles.

"It's kind of green and purple now," quipped Kevin.

"Yes, thank you, Kevin," said Tina, "I haven't forgotten."

Now that Giles thought about it, he wasn't at all sure about having the robot to stay either. Tina's inventions were often unreliable. To be fair, some of them were huge successes, like her ghostometer. But they also had a nasty habit of shrinking things unexpectedly, or making them frizzle up like bits of burnt spaghetti. It was not uncommon for Mr. and Mrs. Quark to ban Kevin and Tina from their basement workshop after a particularly disastrous experiment.

"I thought I heard someone at the door," called out Mr. Barnes, coming in the back door from his workshop.

"It's Tina and Kevin," Giles called back. "And their robot."

There was a brief silence.

"Oh," said Mr. Barnes. "Well, maybe they'd like to come in — all three of them."

The robot was already squeezing past Kevin and Tina into the hallway. It shone its flashlight in Giles's face for a moment, studying him. He was reminded of a visit to the optometrist.

"Did Tina Quark create you as well?" the robot asked in its metallic voice.

"No way!" exclaimed Giles indignantly.

"It asked me that, too," said Kevin sympathetically. "In fact, it's asked everyone that, including Mom and Dad. They were pretty annoyed."

"I bet!" said Giles.

"It's simply curious," said Tina. "It has an inquisitive mind, unlike some people I'm acquainted with," she added, giving Kevin a withering look.

But the robot seemed to have lost interest in Giles and was ambling down the hallway as if it were in a public art gallery. Then it turned and disappeared into the living room.

"Whoa," came Mr. Barnes's voice from around the corner. "What have we here?"

17

Giles ushered Tina and Kevin inside and hurried after the robot.

"I take it, Tina, this is one of your creations," said Mr. Barnes.

"That's right," she replied. "It's the Tinatron 1000."

"They wanted to know if Tinatron could stay here for a few days," Giles said.

Mr. Barnes's gaze fell to the carpet that had once been blue.

"Mr. Barnes," said Tina hurriedly, "you have my assurance that Tinatron is perfectly safe. It won't be any trouble at all."

At that moment, Mrs. Barnes walked into the room. Everyone turned to look at her. Giles drew in his breath sharply. His mother's eyes fixed on the robot for a few moments. Then she glanced quickly over to Tina and Kevin Quark, who were standing rigidly side by side, with huge, hopeful smiles frozen on their faces.

"No," Mrs. Barnes said. "Not on your life."

"Elizabeth," said Giles's father with a smile. "It's a robot orphan. Where's your compassion?"

"I want it out," said Mrs. Barnes with a flinty-eyed stare at Tina. "I want it out before it blows up the house."

For once, Giles was on his mom's side. He couldn't put his finger on it, but there was something about Tinatron that rubbed him the wrong way!

"It's completely out of the question!" said Mrs. Barnes. "I've got a lot of work to do on this new series of math equations, and I won't be interrupted by some walking nine-volt battery!"

While all this was going on, Tinatron had meandered over to the coffee table and was peering intently at the textbook Mrs. Barnes had brought into the room with her.

"The Quintilliax equations are unusually complex," the robot said. "Only those of advanced intelligence are able to solve their many intricacies."

Tina beamed like a proud mother whose baby has just burbled its first words. Mrs. Barnes's mouth fell open slightly. Then a smile spread across her face.

"It can stay," she said.

* * *

"What is that?" asked the robot, pointing at the jumble of plastic pieces on Giles's desk.

"It's a model airplane kit," he explained. "You glue it together. This is going to be the best one yet. It's going to be perfect."

"Those two pieces are crooked," said the robot.

"Yes, well," said Giles, slightly flustered, "I was in a hurry to open the door."

Tinatron stood in the centre of his room, swivelling its head around to take everything in. Giles was at a loss. Robot-sitting! What was he supposed to do with it? Was he supposed to talk to it? Play with it? Somehow he couldn't see this robot rolling dice and plunking a plastic counter around a board. This was a very serious robot.

It had been almost impossible to get Tina to leave. She'd fussed over the robot as if she were sending it away for two years instead of a few days! She'd reminded him of all the proper procedures three or four times, until Kevin had gently but firmly guided her out of the room and out the front door.

"Your drawers are not properly closed," announced Tinatron gravely.

"Yeah, well." Giles slammed shut a few drawers.

"There is an accumulation of dust on your shelves."

"It's always like that!"

"That poster is drooping slightly in the upper right corner."

"So what?"

"It is not perfect."

Giles just looked at the robot.

"Look, you've had a long day," he said. "Why don't you get some sleep?"

"Sleep?" said the robot.

"Oh, right. Should I plug you in, then?"

"My battery does not yet require recharging."

"Well," said Giles, "I've got to do some homework for tomorrow."

"I will do it," said Tinatron immediately.

"No thanks," said Giles. "Besides, it's got to be in my own handwriting, or they'll think I cheated."

"I can copy any style of handwriting," the robot replied. "I am programmed not to make a single mistake."

Giles looked thoughtfully at his model kit. If Tinatron did all his homework, he'd have more time to work on the bomber. It was awfully tempting. And why not? If he had to look after this robot for a few days, why shouldn't he get something out of it? He could hand in flawless homework, too, just like Tina! He could hardly wait to see the look on her face when his marks were called out!

"All right," he told Tinatron. "I'll get the books for you."

Maybe, he thought, this robot-sitting wouldn't be so bad after all.

Chapter 4

Pure Genius

"HOW'S TINATRON?" Tina asked Giles the next morning at school.

"Fine, I guess," Giles replied. It was only a machine, how could you describe how it was?

"Not overheating?" Tina inquired.

"I don't think so, no."

"You plugged it in last night, according to my instructions?"

"I did, and all the lights flickered, and a deep humming sound came from Tinatron's chest. It was a bit freaky."

"That's the high voltage battery!" said Tina grandly. "It's a beautiful creation, don't you think, Barnes?"

A dreamy look had come into her eyes, and Giles looked at Kevin and winked. Tina could get a little carried away sometimes.

"Did you know," she said, "that the word robot comes from the Czech word *robota*?"

"I can't even spell 'Czech,' " commented Kevin.

"Ah! If they could only see now what I've done with that little word of theirs," said Tina. "I've made it come true. I've made the perfect machine!"

"So what are you going to do with it now?" Giles wanted to know.

"I thought that was obvious," said Tina with an impatient scowl. "You know how slow things have been for the genius business lately! Times are tough, Barnes! People are cutting back on geniuses! But the Tinatron 1000 is just what we need to put us back on top! We'll make a fortune! Here, look at this."

She held up the front page of the local newspaper. There was a large photograph of Tina and the robot accepting their award at the science fair, and underneath was a long article. The headline read: "PURE GENIUS!"

"The calls should be pouring in any time now," said Tina with supreme confidence.

"Well, this is good news," said Kevin cheerfully.

"And Tinatron is just the first step," Tina said. "With its help, I'll build a whole battalion of robot workers!"

"*More* robots?" asked Giles. "But why?"

"Why?" said Tina in exasperation. "Barnes, these robots are a hundred times better than people! They're faster, smarter, and they don't get into silly moods! And they never make mistakes. Not one! Mark my words, before long they're going to replace people!"

* * *

When Giles came home after school, he was greeted by the dainty clink of china and the low burble of voices from the living room. He kicked off his muddy running shoes and walked in to have a look.

Giles gaped. It was one of the weirdest things he'd ever seen.

His mother was sitting forward in an armchair, a cup of tea in her hand, chattering away eagerly. Opposite her was Tinatron, reclined comfortably on the sofa, a china cup held delicately between two rubber-glove fingers.

"So the Templehof math formulas are essentially useless?" Mrs. Barnes said.

"Yes," Tinatron replied. "My data is always flawless."

"Remarkable," said Mrs. Barnes. "Just remarkable. You must have incredible skill at mathematics."

"That is correct," said the robot.

Mrs. Barnes and Tinatron were so engrossed in their conversation that they didn't notice Giles at all. He watched, breathless, as the robot lifted the teacup to its metal face as if to drink, but then set it back on its saucer.

"Oh, hello, Giles," said his mother, beaming. "I didn't hear you come in. Tinatron and I are just having a fantastic discussion."

"I see," said Giles tightly.

Obviously Tinatron and his mother had hit it off. There they were, guzzling tea and chatting away like best friends! He didn't like it one little bit, even though he couldn't quite explain why.

"Now then," said Mrs. Barnes, turning back to the robot, "could you go over the Orion equations again?"

"Certainly," said the robot. "It's very straight-forward. Let us begin with — "

Scowling, Giles backed out of the room and thudded up the stairs. In the doorway to his bedroom, he froze. He barely recognized his room.

It had been tidied.

He'd never thought of his bedroom as unusually

messy — he'd seen far worse at some of his friends' houses. But this wasn't just an ordinary tidying up. The bed was so tightly made, you could have used it as a trampoline. There was nothing on the floor — no dirty clothes, no comics or books scattered around. He walked in warily, as if he were afraid of setting off some horrible booby trap.

There wasn't a speck of dust on his shelves. The posters no longer drooped. All his books had been arranged alphabetically. He opened a drawer. His socks had been tightly coiled and arranged by colour. It was frightening.

But what really stopped Giles dead in his tracks was his model airplane kit — the one he'd been doggedly working on for weeks.

The bomber rested in the middle of the desk, completely made, right down to the decals on the wings.

Tinatron!

He rushed back downstairs into the living room.

"You built my model airplane!" he shouted at the robot.

"Giles!" said Mrs. Barnes. "What on earth's the matter?"

"The robot finished my model!"

"It was incomplete," Tinatron replied in its metallic voice. "I completed it for you."

"*I* wanted to complete it!" exclaimed Giles. "That's the whole point! That's the fun of it!"

"Fun?" said the robot. "I am unfamiliar with this word. Please provide me with a concise definition."

"Tinatron was just trying to help," said Mrs. Barnes with a small frown.

"It tidied up my room, too!" said Giles.

"I know," said Mrs. Barnes. "I thought it looked fabulous."

"It is now perfect," said Tinatron.

"I'll never be able to find anything!" said Giles. "I'll need a crowbar to get into my bed!"

Mrs. Barnes didn't seem terribly concerned by any of this.

"You know, Giles," she said, "there are some people at the university who would be very interested in meeting Tinatron. Do you think Tina Quark would mind?"

"I'm sure she'd be thrilled," said Giles grumpily.

His mother never seemed that interested in anything *he'd* done. She hardly even glanced at his model airplanes half the time. But bring a robot home, and she was making it tea and chatting and complimenting it all over the place! It was sickening!

"Mom, why did you make it tea? It's a robot!"

His mother looked thoughtful. "It seemed . . . polite, that's all."

He turned and stormed out of the room.

Chapter 5

The Perfect Machine

GILES STARED LISTLESSLY at his model air-plane. He hadn't hung it up with all the others. He got no satisfaction from looking at it, even if it was perfect. After all, he hadn't built it, had he?

Making models was the one thing he'd always thought he was good at, and now it turned out a robot could do it a hundred times better! Maybe Tina was right — robots would replace people altogether before long!

He sighed. He'd been robot-sitting for five days now. Every afternoon he came home to his perfect bedroom, and every morning he left with his perfect homework. The robot did it all without even asking now. His marks had never been better, but it was just like with the model bomber: it didn't make him feel good at all. He thought he'd enjoy seeing Tina's face when his marks were called out in class, but she only smiled to herself, as if she'd known all along what was going on. It was just another triumph for her robot!

Giles heard a knock at the door and went downstairs to answer it. Kevin stood glumly on the front steps.

"Come in," said Giles. "Where's Tina?"

"Oh, she's in the workshop, drawing up plans for more robots. I don't see her much anymore. Every now and then she comes up for a meal, and looks at me and Mom and Dad and just shakes her head a little sadly, and then goes back downstairs."

"At least you don't have to listen to her talking about what a genius she is," said Giles.

"I guess," said Kevin. "But you know, I actually miss her! Lately she hasn't even bothered telling me what a tiny brain I have! Even that would be better than this silence!"

"Well, if it's any comfort, my mom's fallen in love with Tinatron."

"Really?"

"Yeah. They talk for hours together. Right now

they're in her study, working on some new math equation. Mom's all excited. She keeps saying it's going to be perfect!"

"I bet," said Kevin.

All the lights in the living room suddenly flickered.

"That's Tinatron," said Giles. "Dad says the electricity bills are going to be terrible."

"You know what's really terrible?" said Kevin awkwardly. "Here. This is why I came over."

He fished around in his pocket and handed Giles a crumpled business card.

Tina Quark and Associates.
Local Genius Service.
Capable of absolutely *everything!*
Reasonable Rates.

"She's taken your name off!" Giles exclaimed.

Kevin nodded. "And I don't think I'm one of the associates either."

"But she can't do that!" blustered Giles. "It's not fair!"

"I've been replaced, Barnes — replaced by robots."

Mr. Barnes walked in, carrying a huge sheaf of construction plans.

"You two look pretty low," he said. "What's up?"

"A crazy case of robots," muttered Kevin.

"I think I know what you mean," sighed Mr. Barnes, slumping back on the sofa between the two of them. "Take a look at this."

He spread out the detailed plans for his home renovations. They were covered in precise red scribbles.

"Tinatron," said Giles simply.

"Yes," said Mr. Barnes. "I've been working on these for months, and now I find red pen all over them. The infuriating thing is, the robot's absolutely right."

"Maybe we should just accept it," said Kevin. "Tinatron's better than us."

"Well, I think you're being a little hasty there," said Mr. Barnes. "There's no question machines can do some things faster — and more efficiently — than us, but we're still better at a lot of other things."

All three sat in silence for a few moments.

"I can't think of anything," said Giles. "What about you, Kevin?"

"Completely blank," said Kevin with a defeated shake of his head.

"Well," said Mr. Barnes, "I'm sure if you had a good long think, you'd come up with something!"

"It still doesn't change the fact that I'm not on the business card anymore," said Kevin miserably.

All the lights in the room flickered again. But this time there was a sharp, crackling noise from upstairs. Then the whole house went dark.

Chapter 6

Blowing a Fuse

"WHAT HAPPENED?" said Giles, rushing into his mother's study.

"Are you all right, Elizabeth?" Mr. Barnes asked his wife.

"Fine, fine!" she said impatiently. "It's Tinatron!"

The robot was slumped against the wall, smouldering.

"It said it needed more power to solve the equation," explained Giles's mother breathlessly, "so I plugged it in. Then it started humming, getting louder and louder, and all of a sudden it was shooting out sparks!"

"It looks like it's overloaded itself," said Giles.

"Serves it right," Kevin said. "Show-off."

"What a shame," said Mr. Barnes.

"What are you three grinning about?" cried Mrs. Barnes. "We were right in the middle of making a mathematical breakthrough!"

Secretly Giles wanted to cheer. But he knew it would be no laughing matter if the robot really were damaged and Tina found out. He walked over to Tinatron and flicked a switch at the top of its head, just as Tina had shown him. To his relief, the robot's flashlight eye lit up.

"I wonder if it's all right," said Mrs. Barnes worriedly.

"I am Tinatron 1000," said the robot. "I am the perfect machine."

"Oh, I think it's just fine," said Giles with a mocking smile.

"Ask me any question. I am programmed to answer without error."

"Maybe later," said Giles. He was already sorry he'd turned the robot back on.

"You may make the question as difficult as you wish."

"Two plus two," said Giles in a bored voice, hoping to shut it up.

"Five," said the robot instantly.

Giles blinked and looked at Kevin. Could this be a joke? But robots didn't have a sense of humour. Tinatron certainly didn't — that had been abundantly clear all along.

"Are you sure about that, Tinatron?" Giles asked carefully.

"Yes," said the robot.

"I think," said Giles, "we have a problem."

"It probably didn't hear you," said Kevin. "Tinatron, what's six times six?"

"Forty."

"Oh dear," said Mrs. Barnes softly.

"The answer is thirty-six," said Kevin.

"Let's try something else," Giles suggested. "Tinatron, what colour is Kevin's sweater?"

"Thirty-six?" said the robot hopefully. A few more sparks licked out from its metal frame. It peered down at the papers on Mrs. Barnes's desk.

"What is this?" it asked.

"It's the equation we were just working on!" said Mrs. Barnes.

Tinatron picked up one of the sheets, staring at it intently.

"I know what to do with this," it said.

"You do?" said Mrs. Barnes excitedly.

Everyone waited to see what the robot would say next. With great concentration, Tinatron folded the paper once, then twice. Then it quickly made a whole series of folds, until it held a paper airplane in its rubber-glove hands. The robot sent it gliding across the room.

It's flipped, thought Giles.

"This is a disaster!" said Mrs. Barnes. "We should call Tina right away!"

"Oh, I don't think that's such a good idea," said Kevin quickly.

"Maybe it just needs some time to recover," suggested Giles.

Tinatron squeezed past him and walked into the hallway.

"Look," said Mr. Barnes to Kevin and Giles, "you two keep an eye on it, I'll fix the fuses."

The robot had wandered into Giles's bedroom and was going through the bookshelves, picking out books, glancing at them and then dropping them onto the floor.

"That's a fine model," Tinatron commented. "Did you build it, Barnes?"

"No, you did."

Tinatron picked up the bomber, turning it over in

its hands. One of the wings snapped off.

"Oh dear," said Tinatron.

Giles had never heard a robot say "Oh dear" before. He began to laugh. So did Kevin. So did Tinatron. It came out as a rather odd, metallic, booming noise, but it was laughter all the same.

At that moment, Tina walked in.

She just stood there, looking from Giles to Kevin, then to the robot.

"All right, what have you done to it?" she demanded.

"Well," said Kevin in a faltering voice, "it's like this — "

"Tinatron's had a nasty shock," said Giles. "It overloaded itself while doing a math problem with my mom."

"Impossible," said Tina. "It's programmed not to overload itself. It wouldn't make a mistake like that."

Giles shrugged. "I think it did anyway."

"Are you malfunctioning, Tinatron?" Tina asked.

"Ask me a question. I will give the incorrect answer."

Giles couldn't help smiling. But Tina looked very serious. She opened a small metal hatch in the robot's head and peered inside.

"This is terrible," she muttered. "I don't understand how this could have happened!"

She shut the hatch and looked angrily at the robot.

"You have made a mistake," she said.

"I have made a mistake," echoed the robot.

Tina sighed and turned to Giles. "I'll need to make some major repairs. I don't have the right tools with me now, but I'll be back first thing in the morning. I'd better go to the workshop and get everything ready."

With that, she turned and left the room.

"I have made a mistake," said Tinatron. "I am no longer perfect."

For the first time, Giles almost felt sorry for the robot.

He'd disliked Tinatron from the start, but it wasn't the robot's fault it was so insufferable. It had no real feelings. It was only a machine. It only did what it was programmed to do. And Tina had programmed it to be perfect.

But with a jolt, Giles realized it wasn't just Tina's fault!

His mom wanted the perfect math equation.

His dad wanted the perfect home renovations.

And *he* wanted perfect homework and perfect model airplanes!

It was hardly a surprise that Tinatron blew a fuse! It was just trying to do what everyone really wanted!

But what was so bad about a few mistakes anyway? It wasn't the end of the world if he didn't get 20 out of 20 on all his homework, or his airplane models had a few crooked pieces! He'd tried his very best, and that's all that mattered in the end.

It was impossible to be perfect all the time.

But, Giles wondered, did Tina know that?

Chapter 7

Panicking

"GONE?" SAID TINA.

"Yes," said Giles. "When I woke up this morning, the robot wasn't there. It must have sneaked out in the night."

"Gone?" Tina said again, her eyes wide.

"She'll snap out of it," Kevin whispered to Giles. "She's just a little upset."

"A little upset!" shouted Tina. "My robot has run away, Kevin. How do you think that makes me feel? It must have malfunctioned worse than I thought! It could be anywhere by now!"

"Maybe it's gone south," said Giles. "This damp weather can't be very good for its joints."

Tina turned a stony gaze on him.

"I'm afraid I don't find that amusing, Barnes. This is a HIGHLY SERIOUS MATTER! Anything could have happened to it. It could have been kidnapped by scientists at the university who want my secrets — yes, that's probably it! They read all about me in the paper and now they want the robot for themselves!"

Giles rolled his eyes.

"We've got to find it!" said Tina.

"Us?" said Giles, winking at Kevin. "I don't know, Tina, we're really not genius material."

"My name's not even on the business card anymore," Kevin pointed out.

Tina flushed. "You weren't supposed to see that, Kevin," she mumbled. "It was just an idea I was toying with."

"Well, you certainly don't need us anymore," said Giles. "I mean, what good are we? We're only human after all."

"You know, I sort of like not being part of the genius business," said Kevin, stretching out luxuriously on the sofa. "It gives you a chance to kick up your feet, take a deep breath and enjoy the good things in life."

"Don't be ridiculous," snapped Tina. "You sound

like a margarine commercial! We've got to find Tinatron!"

Giles and Kevin just smiled at her.

"Fine," she said carelessly. "I don't need any help. I never have, have I? It's always me who's done everything! All I need is a good plan . . . " Her voice trailed off as she stood stock still in the middle of the room, staring at the wall. "A plan will come to me at any moment . . . a brilliant plan . . . "

"I think she's panicking," Giles said to Kevin.

"No," said Kevin, "she's a genius. She'll figure something out."

"I've never seen her like this, though," said Giles.

"All right!" exclaimed Tina, wringing her hands. "I'm panicking. I need your help!"

"What about the small matter of those business cards?" said Kevin.

"I'll shred them!" said Tina.

"What do you think?" said Giles to Kevin. "Can you live with that?"

"Well . . . ok!" said Kevin, snapping to his feet. "Let's get cracking!"

Chapter 8

The Hunt

KEVIN MADE A POSTER. He drew a picture of Tinatron, and above it in big letters wrote HAVE YOU SEEN THIS ROBOT?

"Hey, that's really good," said Giles. "I didn't know you could draw like that. You've captured Tinatron exactly!"

"Thanks," said Kevin, a little shyly.

"You missed a bolt on the right of its head," said Tina.

"Oh, put a cork in it!" said Giles. "It's an excellent picture. Who cares about a bolt or two!"

"Shall we get going, then?" said Tina huffily.

After photocopying the poster at the library, they pinned it up outside store windows and phone booths. Then they spent the rest of the day scouring the neighbourhood for signs of Tinatron, showing the poster to everyone they saw.

"I saw it heading east," said a paper boy.

"I saw it heading west," said the mailman.

"I think I saw it talking to a telephone pole," said a girl in the park.

"It walked into my lawn mower," said a man from his front yard.

"It was muttering to itself," said a boy on a bike. "It kept saying, 'I have made a mistake' over and over again."

But not once did Giles, Kevin, and Tina catch a glimpse of Tinatron themselves.

* * *

"I'm wiped out," said Giles, sinking down into the sofa.

"I think I've worn holes in my shoes," said Kevin.

"I just don't understand how the robot could have made a mistake!" said Tina.

"Don't worry," said Giles. "Machines always break down sooner or later."

"I'll just have to try harder next time!" said Tina fiercely to herself. "I know I can do it!"

"It's not so important, is it?" Giles said.

"Look," said Tina, "if we don't find the robot, the genius business is finished! Tinatron and all the others were going to attract lots of customers for us. I don't know what we'll do without them!"

"There must be other ways to get business," said Giles.

The telephone rang and Tina practically flew across the room to grab it.

"Hello? Yes. Yes. That's correct. Yes. Well, thank you very much. I'll be sure to tell my brother, yes."

Giles raised his eyebrows at Kevin. Who was she talking to?

"You have?" shouted Tina into the phone. "You're quite certain? When? Where?" She grabbed for a pad of paper and hurriedly scribbled something on it. "Thank you very much."

She slammed down the phone.

"What was that all about?" Giles asked.

"What were you supposed to tell me?" Kevin wanted to know.

"Never mind that now," snapped Tina. "We've got to hurry! The robot's been sighted. Its battery must have run out. It's been picked up by the metal salvage truck!"

Chapter 9

Crushed

MOUNTAINS OF SCRAP METAL towered up around Giles.

"We'll never find Tinatron in all of this," he said, still out of breath from the long run.

"Yes, we will," said Tina determinedly.

In the distance, a huge metal claw descended from a crane and grabbed a fistful of trash. The claw lifted the scraps high into the air and then dumped them into a machine with a gaping mouth. The mouth closed and there was a terrible crunching sound. Giles shuddered.

"There!" said Kevin, pointing to the top of one of the metal mountains.

Giles squinted. It hardly looked like a robot now,

all crumpled in on itself. And it certainly didn't look like something you would call the perfect machine. It blended in almost completely with the other pieces of scrap metal.

"Thank goodness," said Tina.

But no sooner had she said the words than the huge claw began to slowly swing towards Tinatron.

"No," gasped Tina, her eyes widening. "My robot!"

Before Giles could stop him, Kevin dashed towards the metal mountain and was leaping up its side.

"I'll get it!" he shouted.

"Kevin!" Tina cried out, racing after him. "No!"

"Stop!" Giles yelled.

He could feel the mountain of rusted metal shift beneath his feet as he staggered up, Tina at his side. Kevin had a hold on the robot, but it was too heavy for him to lift by himself.

Giles saw the pincers of the claw opening as it came closer. But Kevin was still stubbornly trying to drag Tinatron down the heap of scrap metal. Giles finally reached him and grabbed hold of his arm.

"Let it go!" Giles shouted.

The metal claw swooped nearer still, casting a

huge shadow over all of them.

"Come on, Kevin!" bellowed Tina, who now gripped her brother's other arm. "Please!"

Kevin let go, and they all lurched headlong down to the ground. The big claw sank its pincers into the robot, lifted it up and dropped it into the metal masher.

"Kevin, why did you do that?" Giles demanded.

"I felt sorry for it, I guess," Kevin said. "Making all those mistakes. I know how it feels."

"It doesn't *feel* anything! It's just a machine!"

"I'm sorry I didn't get there in time," Kevin said to his sister.

"Kevin," she shouted, "don't you ever do anything so stupid again!"

"But it was so important to you!" he shouted back.

"Not as important to me as you are!" she shouted, and then looked a little confused. "Not anywhere near as important!"

"Could have fooled me," said Kevin.

"I'm sorry," said Tina. "It's just that I worked so hard on that robot."

"I don't mind sharing the business with a robot or two," said Kevin, "as long as I don't get replaced altogether."

"There won't be any robots at all," said Tina firmly. "We don't need them now anyway. Remember the man who called about the robot? Well, he'd seen the poster, and he liked your drawing so much he wants to hire the genius business to do some work for him."

"Really?" said Kevin.

"So the genius business will go on!" said Giles.

"Without robots!" said Kevin.

Tina nodded. "It was a stupid idea of mine. A very stupid idea."

"Don't worry," said Kevin, throwing his arm around her shoulders. "Nobody's perfect. Not even you."

Kenneth Oppel's first book, *Colin's Fantastic Video Adventure*, was published when he was fifteen years old. Since then he has written sixteen more books, including the best-selling novels *Silverwing* and *Sunwing*, both of which have won the Mr. Christie's Book Award and the Canadian Library Association's Book of the Year for Children Award.

Kenneth lives in Toronto with his wife and two children. Visit his website at: *http://members.aol.com/kenoppel*

The first exciting
Barnes and the Brains adventure!

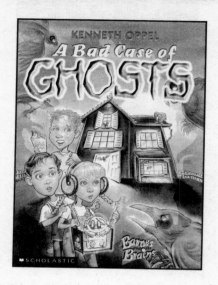

Giles Barnes and his family have just moved — into a
very strange house. Creaks, rustles, and fluttering
sounds fill his bedroom. His mother insists there is no
such thing as ghosts, but Giles decides to investigate.
He enlists the help of his new neighbours, "local
geniuses" Tina and Kevin Quark, and their
"ghostometer," and together Barnes and the Brains
solve the mystery — and get rid of the ghosts for good!

A Bad Case of Ghosts
by Kenneth Oppel
ISBN 0-590-51750-3
$4.99

Barnes and the Brains, back on the case!

When Giles, Tina and Kevin see books moving in the library, all by themselves, they know they have to investigate. But Tina's amazing ghostometer doesn't pick up any ghosts, so what could that mysterious presence be? Nobody expects what they actually find — and once again, it takes a dose of Giles's own common-sense magic to get things back to normal.

A Strange Case of Magic
by Kenneth Oppel
ISBN 0-439-98732-6
$4.99